This book belongs to:

_____

**Other books by Patsy Smith Roberts:**

- *Rory, The Adventures of a Lion Cub*
- *Kabelo, The Adventures of a Baby Giraffe*
- *Willis the Warthog*

To order online, visit our website:
www.patsysmithroberts.com.

# NIGEL

## The adventures of a baby elephant

*and his meerkat friend* MOE

*2012*

For Yvonne —
My Africa —
to You!
Best Wishes,
Patsy S. Roberts

Photography and Story by Patsy Smith Roberts

Published by Savuti Muti Publishing

## WEBSITE & PURCHASING INFORMATION

www.patsysmithroberts.com

P.O. Box 22096
St. Simons Island, GA 31522 – USA

Published by:

Savuti Muti Publishing
P.O. Box 22096
St. Simons Island, Georgia 31522

Printed in China

ISBN 978-0-9758599-2-6

Second Printing

## Acknowledgments:

*Whatever it was that drew me to Africa that first time remains a mystery to me even after 20 trips. There are memories from Africa that I hold close to my heart – hearing the lions roar at night and being in the bush camps with the staff who never fails to make me know that I am home.*

*The Botswana Government is to be commended for the fine job it does with its conservation program. I always know what a privilege it is to see those magnificent animals in their natural habitat.*

*A special thank you to my friend, Sandy Fowler, who always manages to find a spare tent for me at Orient Express Safari camps; and to Becky Parker, who has the difficult task of working with me designing the book.*

*This book would never have come together without all the suggestions from friends, who are my editors and assistant editors. David, Barbara, Betty Sue, Gerry, Mimi, Margo, Sue, and Wade, thank you for what you added to the book and especially for what you add to my life. Living with Nigel, Moe, and me this past year has not been easy!*

*For all the "little readers" who buy my books, Margo and I thank you from the bottoms of our hearts!*

*PATSY SMITH ROBERTS*

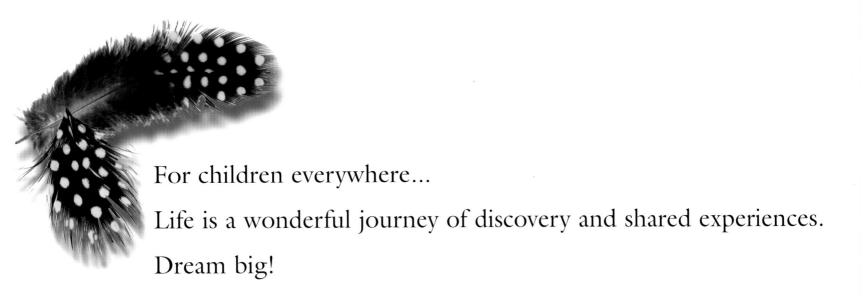

For children everywhere...

Life is a wonderful journey of discovery and shared experiences.

Dream big!

P.S.R.

One afternoon in the African country of Botswana, a baby elephant named Nigel and his Mum were walking to the river.

The feeling of her trunk across his back made him feel so safe.

Suddenly… Nigel heard loud gunshots!

Some illegal hunters, called poachers, had come to the savanna, and now Nigel's Mum was gone.

He ran and hid for days under an acacia bush... grieving for his Mum. Nigel knew that now he would have to try to survive on his own.

As he slowly left the protection of the acacia bush, he startled a small creature digging nearby. Looking up into Nigel's sad eyes, the creature knew that something terrible had happened.

"Hey... what's wrong?" the small, furry creature asked.

"Who are you?" Nigel asked.

"I'm just a meerkat named Moe. **Who are you?**" the saucy meerkat asked.

"My name is Nigel. I've lost my Mum and I'm scared. She warned me about the Savuti lions that live here."

Moe said, "Don't worry... there's a herd of elephants that lives down the river, and I'll help you find them. I'm sure that Eleanor, the female in charge, will let you join her herd."

"Leave it to me," added Moe, confidently. "My cousin was a tour guide here, so I know my way around this part of the African bush."

"It'll be a **dangerous** journey. We'd better leave now.

"Those Savuti lions will begin to hunt when it gets dark," Moe added.

They had walked for several miles when Moe quickly stopped.

"See those two lion cubs hiding in the grass? Their Mum will be returning soon. We need to **hurry**."

"Moe, I'm thirsty. Is there a place we can get some water?" Nigel asked.

"Maybe we can stop at Pump Pan. I'll check to see if it's safe," Moe said.

But as they got nearer, Moe saw two lionesses and their cubs drinking at the pan. He **knew** there was not a chance to get water there.

Just when it seemed there was no place to get a drink, they ran into Grace, the gentle giraffe, who just happened to overhear them.

"Hey, fellows, I think I can help. I've seen elephants stripping bark from the Baobab tree to gather its moisture. Look, there's one right over there!" she said.

**N**igel quickly stripped off enough bark to satisfy his thirst because he knew they had to keep going.

They hadn't gone far when an animal with no tail ran by.

"Who's that without a tail?" Nigel asked.

Moe stood on his little hind legs to check.

"That's Willis, the bravest warthog I know," said Moe. "He lost his tail to Leroy the Leopard while saving his little sister's life. Now come on, Nigel. We need to keep going or something **bad** could happen to us."

Closer to the river, they saw a huge animal with skin the color of Nigel's. "We must be getting near the river... I see an elephant over there," Nigel said.

Moe just shook his head, "Don't you know a rhino when you see one? That's Sergeant, and he can be a problem when he's in a bad mood.

"My cousin told me he's been ramming vehicles lately. We need to get out of here! It'll be dark soon, so let's find a safe place to rest for the night."

It wasn't long before they came to an area covered with thick acacias. Nigel and Moe wandered through the thorny bushes until they found a good hiding place to settle in for a long, scary night.

Hours later, as day began to break, a familiar sound woke Nigel.

"Moe... get up!" he shouted. "I can hear elephants far, far, away."

"I don't hear anything," Moe said, his tiny ears twitching.

"But we elephants are special. We can hear for miles. Come on… let's go… I know they're close by," Nigel exclaimed.

And sure enough they soon saw the herd gathered near the river.

At last, Nigel and Moe thought they had arrived safely.

But... things changed very quickly.

**S**uddenly a **raging**, **stomping** creature was **kicking** sand on them.

Nigel was very frightened.

"Who's that? Do you think he will hurt us?"

"**N**o," Moe answered hesitantly. "That's just Buster the Bully showing off for the others and trying to scare us.

"But he can be **trouble** spelled with a capital T. Bullies aren't worth being around. Let's just walk away."

Then something happened that stopped Buster in his tracks.

There was a trumpeting sound...

unlike any Nigel had ever heard.

Standing right in front of them was Eleanor, the matriarch of the herd.

As Buster raced away in panic, Eleanor moved slowly over to comfort Nigel.

"Are you lost?" she asked him gently.

Nigel then told her what had happened to his Mum.

Eleanor drew him near with her trunk and said,
"I am so sorry about what happened to your Mum. That is an example of what happens when animals and humans don't share the world with each other. We all need to come up with some solutions soon.

"Humans can be our **greatest enemy** but also our **only hope** for survival.

"The answer is in their hands."

As Eleanor continued to hold him close, she whispered in his ear the best news of all.

"I want you to be part of my herd," she told him. "I'll be your new Mum… and you'll even have a brother named Baruti!"

With all these exciting things happening to him, Nigel realized he had completely forgotten about Moe.

Where was his wonderful friend who had helped him find his way?

He looked around and saw that Moe was still there, watching. With his eyes, Nigel silently asked Moe to stay.

But Moe knew that he couldn't stay. He hoped the shadows of the leaves would hide his eyes because he never liked for anyone to see him cry.

Bravely, Moe said,
   "Well, I'd better be getting back to the desert. My Mum, Dad, and cousins will be afraid I'm stuck in a hole somewhere. But I'm really going to miss you!"

Nigel sadly replied,
   "Thanks for everything, Moe. I know we are different, but you are the best friend a baby elephant could ever have."

With that, Moe raced away, but with a heavy heart.

A t last, Nigel had a home.

Eleanor gently said to Nigel,

"Let's go find Baruti. He's going to be the happiest one of us all!"

Nigel knew he had found a family that loved him when Baruti reached over and held his trunk as they walked to the river.

**A**nd Moe?

"He's back!" yelled his cousin, standing alert on sentry duty.

Moe's family raced out to meet him!!!

And as the sun set on the beautiful Kalahari Desert, Moe told them all about his new friend Nigel.

Then he smiled to himself. Moe knew that like Nigel, he was home.

# Did You Know?

- A group of elephants is called a herd.
- The female elephant who rules the herd is called the Matriarch.
- Elephants have the same life expectancy as humans and share many of the same emotions. They have a strong sense of family and grieve over lost loved ones, even shedding tears and suffering depression.
- Elephants reach adulthood at the age of 20.
- Elephants have a memory that surpasses humans and spans their lifetime.
- Elephants communicate with incredible long-range infrasound frequencies *(sounds too low for humans to hear);* such sophisticated hearing that even a footfall is heard far away.
- Elephants cool themselves by flapping their ears.
- Elephants are the largest land mammals.
- Pump Pan is a man-made watering hole in the Savuti region of Botswana.

- The meerkat is a small mammal and a member of the mongoose family. It inhabits all parts of the Kalahari Desert in southern Africa.
- A group of meerkats is called a "mob" or "gang."
- Meerkats have a body length of 10-14 inches and an added tail length of 7-10 inches.
- Meerkats are primarily insectivores, but they also eat lizards, snakes, spiders, plants, eggs, and small mammals.
- The Kalahari Desert is a large arid to semi-arid sandy area in southern Africa, covering much of Botswana, parts of Namibia and South Africa.
- The Baobab tree can grow over 130 feet in diameter and is estimated to live up to 4,000 years. Their leaves are rich in Vitamin C and store incredible volumes of water, both in their wood and in hollows in their trunks.

*Patsy at home with Margo.*

Patsy Smith Roberts' first trip to Africa in the early 1990s ignited a passion for the continent as well as for wildlife photography. During her visits to elementary schools, she educates and entertains the students with African stories, photographs, and artifacts. Patsy, a self-taught photographer, lives on St. Simons Island, GA.

Her first children's book was *Rory, The Adventures of a Lion Cub,* which she published and illustrated with her photographs in 2002. Her other books include *Kabelo, The Adventures of a Baby Giraffe* (2004), and *Willis the Warthog* (2005). She is a member of the Society of Children's Writers and Illustrators. For more information, visit the website at www.patsysmithroberts.com.

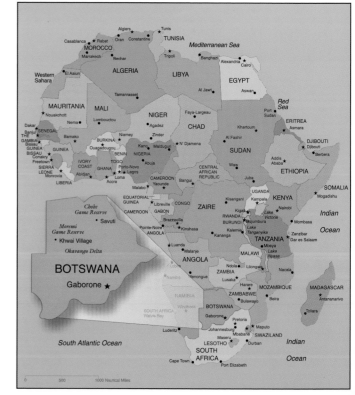